For Roberta Hazel

American edition published in 2020 by Andersen Press USA,
an imprint of Andersen Press Ltd.
www.andersenpressusa.com

First published in Great Britain in 2020 by Andersen Press Ltd.,
20 Vauxhall Bridge Road, London SW1V 2SA.

Distributed in the United States and Canada by
Lerner Publishing Group, Inc.
241 First Avenue North
Minneapolis, MN 55401 USA

For reading levels and more information, look up this title at www.lernerbooks.com.

Color separated in Switzerland by Photolitho AG, Zurich.
Printed and bound in Malaysia

Library of Congress Cataloging-in-Publication Data Available
ISBN: 978-1-72842-410-1

1–TOPPAN–9/1/2020

ELMER
and the
LOST TREASURE

David McKee

Andersen Press USA

Elmer, the patchwork elephant, was with his cousin Wilbur and three other elephants.
"Good morning," called Tiger. "Where are you going so bright and early?"
"On a long, exploring walk," said Elmer.
"Well, I'm having a long, exploring dream," said Lion.

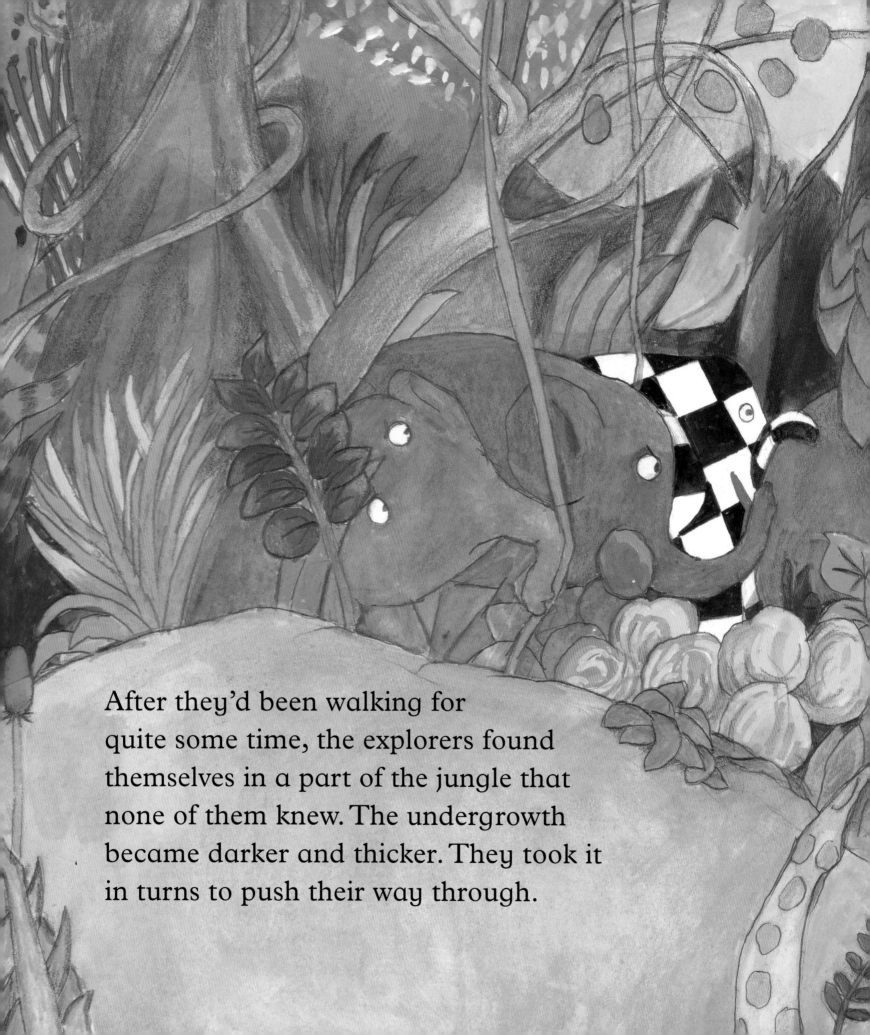

After they'd been walking for
quite some time, the explorers found
themselves in a part of the jungle that
none of them knew. The undergrowth
became darker and thicker. They took it
in turns to push their way through.

Elmer was leading when, with a loud, "Oooh!" he disappeared.
The others stopped and stared.
"Elmer!" they called. "Are you all right?"

Elmer's voice came back. "I'm fine. Come on down.
Be careful—it's a steep slope."

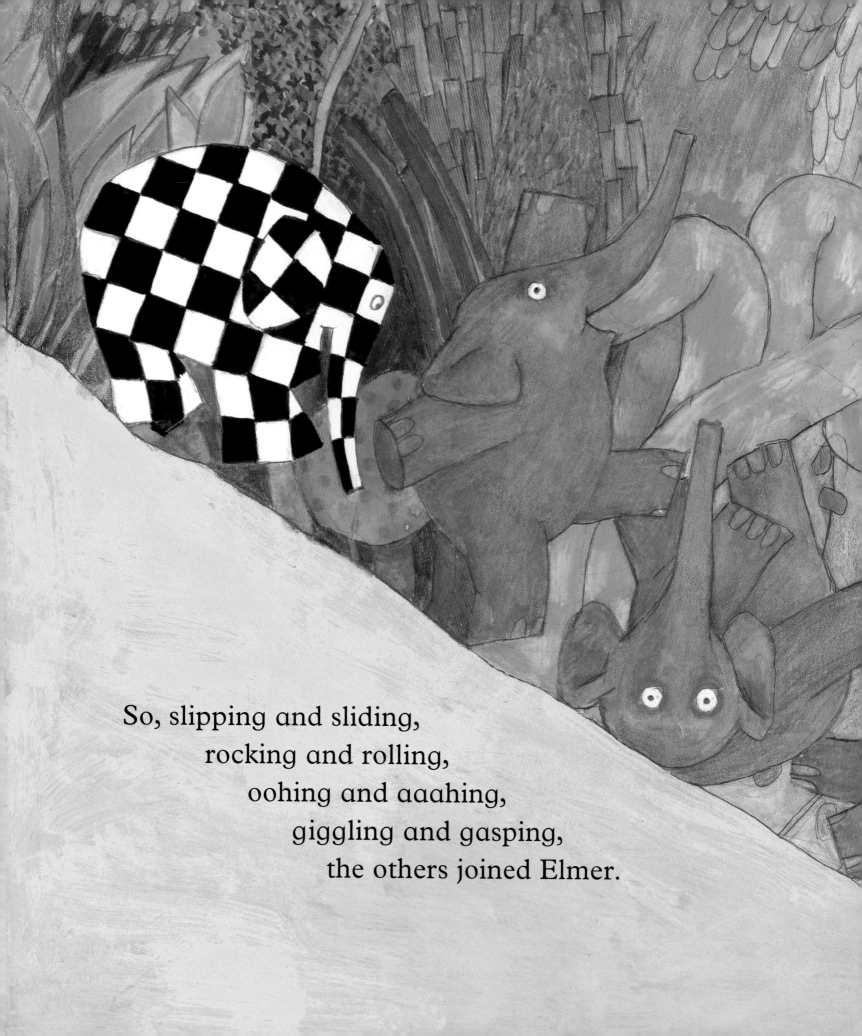

So, slipping and sliding,
rocking and rolling,
oohing and aaahing,
giggling and gasping,
the others joined Elmer.

Once they'd recovered, Elmer said,
"Now, come and see this."
He led them through a curtain of plants.
"Look," he said, and there was the
entrance to a kind of palace.
"WOW!" said the elephants.

"What are we waiting for?" said Wilbur. "Let's take a look." He and Elmer went through the door.

One elephant held the others back and said, "The famous Lost Treasure of the jungle must be hidden here. Don't tell Elmer—we'll find it and surprise him."

Elmer and Wilbur were admiring a large hall when the others scuttled past in the side corridors.

"What are they playing?" said Elmer.
"Probably hide-and-seek," said Wilbur.

A little later, Elmer and Wilbur were surprised to see the elephants standing one on the other. The top elephant was searching the head of a wooden sculpture.
"We thought we saw something," one explained.
"Fascinating," said Elmer.

Soon after that, the cousins were admiring some mosaics and wall paintings when the others sneaked past on tiptoe.

"Stranger and stranger," said Elmer.

"And stranger," added Wilbur.

The next time the other elephants were seen, they were
standing in a dry fountain.
"What are you looking for?" Elmer asked.
    "Oh!" said the elephants in surprise. "Oh! We were ah . . .
        wondering if the fountain still worked."

"There's a lever here," said Elmer as he pulled it.
"Shower time."
Wilbur chuckled. "I think we should be heading home," he said.
"You're right," said Elmer.
"Time to go!" they called to the others.

On the way home, an elephant said, "That was a fun day. Pity we didn't find the Lost Treasure." Elmer and Wilbur stared. "We thought you knew— the whole place was the Lost Treasure."